For my sisters three
Anne,
Jane,
and
Sue
and for little Isaac, too

Copyright © 2003 by Martha Alexander

First edition 2003

Library of Congress Cataloging-in-Publication Data

Alexander, Martha G.
I'll never share you, Blackboard Bear / Martha Alexander. —1st ed.
p.   cm.
Summary: After the bear he has drawn on the blackboard comes to life, Anthony
does not want to share him with Gloria and Stewart.
ISBN 0-7636-1590-0
[1. Bears—Fiction. 2. Sharing—Fiction. 3. Drawing—Fiction.] I. Title.
PZ7.A3777 In 2003
[E]—dc21   2001058120

2 4 6 8 10 9 7 5 3

Printed in Italy

This book was typeset in Stempel Schneidler Roman.
The illustrations were done in colored pencil and watercolor.

Candlewick Press
2067 Massachusetts Avenue
Cambridge, Massachusetts 02140

visit us at www.candlewick.com

I'll Never Share You, BLACKBOARD BEAR

Martha Alexander

CANDLEWICK PRESS
CAMBRIDGE, MASSACHUSETTS

I'm bored. There's nothing to do around here.

Go for a walk? Good idea.

Hi, Anthony. Are you taking your bear out to play?

You're so lucky to have a bear. I want one too.

There are NO more bears like mine, Gloria.
He is the only one in the whole world.

Well, Anthony, I have hundreds of toys.
I'll trade you all of them for your bear.

No, Gloria! My bear says NO, NO, NO.

What's going on here, Gloria?

Oh hi, Stewart. I want to trade Anthony
all my toys for his bear but he won't trade.

I want a bear like that too, Anthony.
Where did you get him?

There are no more bears like mine
in the world. And you can't have him.

Just you wait, Anthony. I might steal him when you're not looking.

Bully, bully, Stewart. My bear wouldn't let you. We're leaving now. Goodbye!

You'll see, Anthony. I'll get him. I'm bigger than you and I'm not afraid of your bear either.

Let's follow them, Stewart.

Gloria, that bear is getting on the blackboard!
Oh, my gosh — he looks just LIKE the blackboard!

Hey, what are you two
doing out there?

I saw your bear getting on the blackboard.
Your secret is out. You DREW that bear.

So what!

Then you can draw one for ME.

And me too, Anthony.
Please, please, please!

My bear wants to talk to me. Come back later.

Share? Why? But you're mine.
How do you know they feel left out?
Well, yes, I would too, I guess.

You have an idea? Sure, try it.

Close your eyes.

We have a surprise.

Oh, Anthony, what a beautiful saddle.
It's awesome.

And you're awesome too, Anthony.

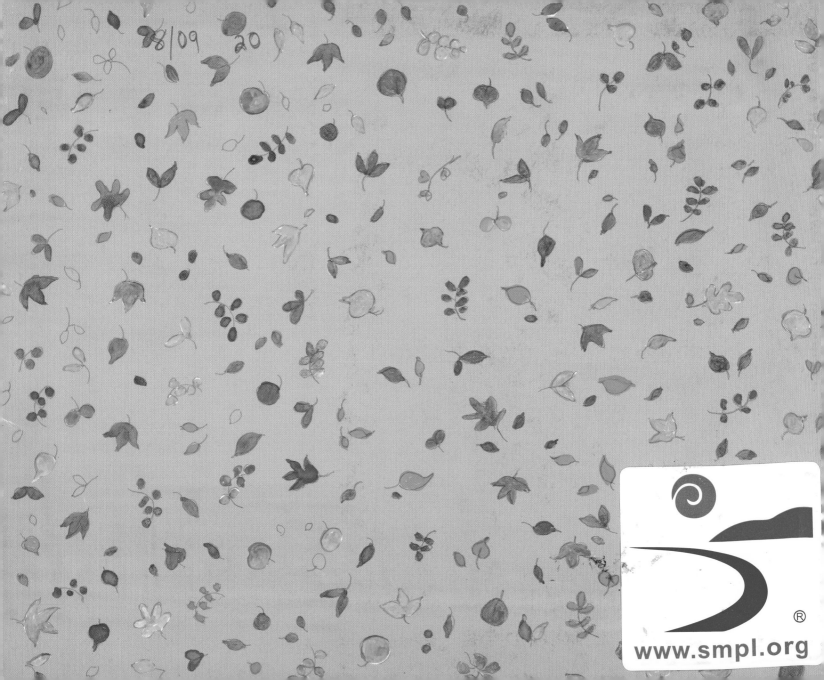